Henry C. Jarrett, Henry D. Palmer

Leo and Lotos

A grand spectacle and romantic fairy drama, in four acts & sixteen

tableaux

Henry C. Jarrett, Henry D. Palmer

Leo and Lotos
A grand spectacle and romantic fairy drama, in four acts & sixteen tableaux

ISBN/EAN: 9783337223021

Printed in Europe, USA, Canada, Australia, Japan

Cover: Foto ©Andreas Hilbeck / pixelio.de

More available books at **www.hansebooks.com**

LEO

and

LOTOS

𝔄 𝔊𝔯𝔞𝔫𝔡 𝔖𝔭𝔢𝔠𝔱𝔞𝔠𝔩𝔢 𝔞𝔫𝔡 ℜ𝔬𝔪𝔞𝔫𝔱𝔦𝔠 𝔉𝔞𝔦𝔯𝔶 𝔇𝔯𝔞𝔪𝔞,

IN FOUR ACTS & SIXTEEN TABLEAUX.

———————

WRITTEN AND ARRANGED EXPRESSLY FOR

NIBLO'S GARDEN, NEW YORK, 1872.

———————

Entered according to Act of Congress, by JARRETT & PALMER,
of Niblo's Garden, New York, ~~September~~, 1872.

Characters in First Act.

PLUTUS (*God of Mammon*) ... ...

ELECTRA (*Ariel à-la-mode*) ... ...

SATANELLA (*the Beautiful Fiend*) ...

SNOWFLAKE (*the Guardian Spirit*) ...

PRINCE LEO (*a Hero of Romance*) ...

THE ASTRONOMER-ROYAL ...

THE POET LAUREATE ... ...

THE GRAND HEREDITARY MUDDLE

PRINCESS LOTOS-LEAF ... ...

BABETTE (*Daughter of Huberlu*) ...

FIDELIO (*the pet Page of Leo*) ... ...

HUBERLU (*retired Sorcerer*) ... ...

GOBO (*Groom to Leo*) ... ...

KING JEWEL (*a precious Potentate*) ...

QUEEN JEWEL (*a very large Stone*) ...

DULCET (*the Jewel Herald*) ... ...

Suzanne, Margot, Berthe, Marotte, Jacqueline (*Sisters to Babette*);
Puff, Opera Box, Cascadette, Carte d'Or, Les Courses (*Spirits*);
*Aurororœ of the North, Bullion Fiends, Infernal Small Change,
Huntsmen, Royal Bicyclist Grooms, Jewel Guards, Jewel Courtiers
and Ladies.*

GRAND BALLET OF JEWELS.

OVERTURE.

ACT I.

SCENE FIRST (*set*).—*The Halls of Mammon.*

PLUTUS *in Council, surrounded by his* GOLD FIENDS, SPRITES, &c.; *picture to open Scene;* ALL *bowed towards the enthroned* PLUTUS, *and to break up on last bars of Chorus.*

[TAKE IN No. 1.]

PLUTUS. We greet ye, minions of Mammon! On the Five thousandth Annual Congress of our Ministers and People, it is satisfactory to find that the world still worships the Calf of Gold with undiminished fervor. (IMP *presents scroll emblazoned in red*) Yes—we see that to-day the potentates of earth have presented their customary homage. Our worship is more universal than ever. Even war ends now in a money claim. Honour is salved by our ministration, and Mammon—Mammon—Mammon—is men's one end and aim.

IMP. All hail, great Plutus! but may it please you, one prince has failed this day to pay his homage.

OMNES. Ah!

PLUTUS. Who is the recreant? (*looking down scroll*)

IMP. Leo, Prince of Gaul.

PLUTUS. (*furious*) How now! Is our power to fail through the incapacity of our minions? Was not his education entrusted to cabinet-ministers devoted to our service?

IMP. True, O Plutus, the Astronomer-Royal, the Poet Laureate, the Grand Hereditary Muddle, were deputed to bring him up in your faith!

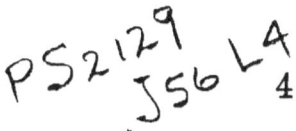

PLUTUS. And they have failed ?

IMP. It would so seem.

PLUTUS. Let them be called! Let the imbeciles be called!
(*Music—a phrase of the opening chorus in orchestra only—
all the performers on the stage are to be moved here quickly
into entirely new picture*)

Enter simultaneously, preceded by SPRITES, R. U. E., *the*
ASTRONOMER-ROYAL, *the* LAUREATE, *and the* GRAND
HEREDITARY MUDDLE—*they advance and bow to* PLUTUS—
Music stops, with chord ff.

So miscreants, ye have failed in your duties ?

THE THREE. Alas ! (*wig business*)*

PLUTUS. Explain how it is I do not number your young
Prince among my vassals ?

ASTRON. We cannot tell. I have cast his horoscope so
subtly that nobody, including myself, could make it out ; and
yet it has thrown no light upon the subject. I have consulted
the stars—yes, even after dinner, in order to see a greater
number—and that too is profitless. I pass.

PLUTUS. And you, O Hereditary Grand Muddle, diplomatist
and statesman, what have you done?

MUDDLE. All. I have reared his youthful mind on Congress
reports. I have provided him Erie statistics to soothe his
leisure hours. I have given him the city records to imbue
him with a desire to become one of your votaries. In vain.
Mining shares, U.S. bonds, even the resumption of specie
payments next century, and a verbatim account of the Geneva
Arbitration have failed to interest my unhappy Prince. I
pass. (*wig business*)

PLUTUS. And you, O Poet Laureate, have your music and
verses failed to produce their effect?

LAUR. Wonderful to relate, they have. Cunningly did I
manœuvre in your service, O Plutus. I even got up a Jubilee,
and pretended it was for Art, when it was only for Mammon.
But it didn't pay, and the Prince did laugh me to scorn. I pass.

---

* The HEREDITARY GRAND MUDDLE has a large fluffy white
wig, practicable, on scalp, and the LAUREATE has a perfectly bare
scalp without hair at all. The business, through the piece, is, for
the MUDDLE in moments of vexation, to pull a handful of hair out
of his wig, and throw it on the stage. The LAUREATE carefully
picks up each lock, and on his next appearance, you find he has
put the lock on his own skull. This goes on regularly, till in the
last scene, the GRAND MUDDLE has become perfectly bald, and the
LAUREATE has a fine white wig. Or it may be simplified by the
LAUREATE keeping all the locks till last act, and then appearing
in the wig.

PLUTUS. Imbeciles! Idiots! Incapables!

THE THREE. Your majesty appears to refer to me.

PLUTUS. Not even fit to be secretaries of state. What do they merit? (*to his* COURT)

OMNES. Death! (*gong—the* THREE *kneel*)

PLUTUS. No; under my reign I have a worse punishment than that. Let them be made bankrupts!

THE THREE. Spare us, great king!

PLUTUS. On one condition. If I find that some occult reason, unknown to men, has interfered with my schemes and your obedience—(*calling*) Come hither, my faithful sprite, my flashing fiend—Electra! (*flash of lightning—a violin rush in the orchestra terminating with chord tutti and cymbals*)

ELECTRA *arises* C. *of stage by trap—the three* MINISTERS *rise.*
Picture.

ELECT. (*saluting with hands over head*) Hail, O master!

PLUTUS. Prompt spirit, whither from?

ELECT. Everywhere.

PLUTUS. Your answer is precise. Know, Electra, that we are in a difficulty? We have been debating——

ELECT. Pardon, sire, I am posted.

PLUTUS. How?

ELECT. As the spirit of Telegraphy, I am cognisant of everything, and perhaps you are not aware that a report of this meeting is being wired to the " New York Herald."

OMNES. Ha! Treachery!

PLUTUS. No matter, useless to war with that paper. We must submit, or they will send down Stanley.

ELECT. You wish to know the power that disputes empire with you in the mind of Prince Leo?

PLUTUS. Rightly conjectured.

ELECT. Nothing more easy.

PLUTUS. (*to three* MINISTERS) Listen, idiots. You hear— nothing more easy.

ASTRON. (*desperately*) Oh! of course not, if you put it in that way. I always knew the prince was fond of yachting.

ELECT. (*laughing*) No, no! Quite idi-yacht-ic!

MUDDLE. Of course not—it was billiards.

ELECT. Wrong again. (*wig business*)

LAUR. Certainly he is wrong. The Prince's soul is wrapped up in theatricals—ballet. (*spins round and stops on one leg*)

ELECT. Nonsense!

PLUTUS. And besides, O incompetent minions, don't you see that Mammon lurks in all these pursuits. No, not such is my foe. What is it, Electra, that thus baffles my power?

ELECT. Listen!

[TAKE IN No. 2.]

SATANEL. Sire, you called me.

PLUTUS. I did, oh, splendid fiend. A horrid rumour breaks our peace—a direful news is like to thwart our power, and bring thee, too, into contempt of mortals. (*with solemnity*) They do say, oh Satanella, that on earth a woman loves, and purely!

SATANEL. Never!

PLUTUS. So said I, but they bring proof of their news.

SATANEL. Fear not, sire. It cannot be. I reign over boudoir and ball room, and I know it cannot be.

ASTRON. (*aside*) A woman's thoughts about women.

MUDDLE. (*aside*) And of course charitable.

(*Music—during next speech the chorus of No. 2 is repeated ppp. in orchestra as in a melodrame*)

SATANEL. True, there was an old legend that, when thy power and mine, O Plutus, were greatest, there should be born a Princess, who in the midst of flattery and pride and circumstance, should love purely and be loved in return by a Prince as child-like as herself. And it was foretold that their high ensample should revive the dead worship of true love, and paralyse the power of Mammon. But I watched my time. The Princess was born—but she was not reared in palaces. I took her, and in the peasant's hut where I placed her, little fear, O Plutus, that the fabled Prince will ever track her or find her. (*music stops*)

PLUTUS. Her name?

SATANEL. Lotos-leaf.

OMNES. Ah!

ELECT. Did I deceive you, master?

PLUTUS. Then is the prophecy fulfilled.

SATANEL. Fulfilled?

PLUTUS. Aye! for the fabled Prince *has* tracked her and *has* found her! (*chord and general exclamation*) What is to be done? Astronomony indicates nought.

ASTRON. Nothing! Correct. (*first looking through theodolite, up*)

PLUTUS. Diplomacy is worse than useless.

MUDDLE. (*humbly*) It always *has* been. (*wig business*)

PLUTUS. And as for Poetry— pah!

LAUR. My own sentiments exactly.

PLUTUS. Therefore, (*to* SATANELLA) beautiful fiend, thine be the task to corrupt the young Prince. This baneful thing, this pure love, must be put a stop to promptly.

SATANEL. It shall be done! Behold my fascinations, my seductions! (*beckoning her nymphs*) Essence of Paris. of Berlin, of Vienna, epitomised for the use of youth. Here's for my Prince—opera box, races; for my Princess—the

fashions, and the cosmetic; for both, the delirium of wine and revelry. (*each in turn pirouettes and salaams*) Reign undisturbed in thy royal despotism, O Plutus, for money shall yet rule Love!

ASTRON. (*aside*) I shouldn't mind going in for a course of temptation myself. (*theodolites them*).

(*Picture forms for finale*, PLUTUS *rising from throne*)*

[TAKE IN No. 3.]

SCENE SECOND.—(*Cloth in 1st*)—*Snowflake's Cool Grot.*

Enter SNOWFLAKE.

SNOW. (*looking at her watch*) Eight o'clock in the morning, and my snow nymphs not returned from earth yet. This is too ridiculous. That stupid old sun has got past his work. Time was, that he exhaled all my snow-spirits up again to their native skies, long before I had come down to breakfast. (*light pizzicato music pp. in orchestra*) Ah! *à la bonne heure!*

The SNOW-SPIRITS *come whirling in* R. *and* L., *form picture, and salute all very quickly.*

Well, young people, better late than never; but let me tell you, that all well-conducted Auroræ of the North, Snowflakes, and other young persons of the upper circles, are expected to keep better hours!

OMNES. Oh, but we've been so busy!

SNOW. (*smiling*) Indeed!

1ST SPIRIT. Yes, there has been a run on iced drinks lately.

2ND SPIRIT. I have been doing the cool in certain political affairs.

3RD SPIRIT. I have been helping to get up a sham Wenham Lake Ice Company, in London.

4TH SPIRIT. And I have been cooling catawba-cup for King Plutus.

SNOW. Ah! what news from Mammon-Ville?

4TH SPIRIT. Oh! a terrible fuss over some recreant Prince, who has been rash enough to renounce allegiance to King Plutus, and fall in love.

OMNES. Ha, ha! the idea!

SNOW. I can well understand, his Majesty doesn't relish that much.

4TH SPIRIT. Not at all: so Satanella——

* For picture to close in, no dance, but a tableau expressive of homage to *King Plutus.*

morning when I was taking up the Prince's shaving-water, I heard him say to his page Fidelio (I don't like pages. What do princes want with pages? Why can't they be satisfied with an attendant like me?) I heard him say, "Fidelio," he said with a sigh, (*imitating*) just like that—"Fidelio, I love a peasant girl. "Who is she?" says the page—like his impudence. "I don't know," says the Prince, "but she lives at the foot of the Sorcerer's Cliff." You might have knocked me down with a feather, for that's where Babette lives, and considering that Babette is engaged to me, you can fancy what my feelings must be. I upset the hot water over the page, and haven't been myself since; no more has he. Let me reflect! (*business*) If I could only see some of the girls.

(BABETTE *and* SISTERS, *off*, *sing together a* "Tra la la" *refrain, which they keep up till they are on*)

There they come from the wood! Now to know the truth.

Enter, L., *the* SISTERS, *dancing and singing, except* BABETTE.

OMNES. O here's a man!

(*they go furiously embracing* GOBO—*business*)

Enter BABETTE, *running*, L.—*she pulls them away.*

BABET. Respect private property, will you?

OMNES. Oh, selfish thing.

BABET. My Gobo!

GOBO. My Babette! (*they embrace*) Then you are faithful still?

BABET. What do you mean?

GOBO. You wouldn't go flirting with princes, would you, eh?

BABET. Like a shot!

OMNES. (*clapping*) So would I!

GOBO. Despair. Let me reflect. (*business*)

BABET. But there aren't any princes to flirt with. (*horns off*)

GOBO. (*groaning*) He's coming, that's clear.

BABET. Who?

GOBO. My master; Prince Leo.

OMNES. O how nice!

GOBO. (*piteously*) Oh, is it, though! When a poor fellow like me sets his youthful affections on you, and then a Prince comes along, and says, "I like your girl; I guess I'll spark her myself."

BABET. Did he say that?

GOBO. He did. Iniquitous—wasn't it?

BABET. Well, it may be iniquitous, and it may not; but my mind's made up; don't seek to disturb the maiden's mind that's made up. I'll go for the Prince myself.

OMNES. And so will I!

GOBO. Ah, you wouldn't feel easy with him, I tell you. He's accustomed to silks and satins, and high-heeled boots, and chignons and waterfalls, and other luxuries.

BABET. Oh, these come naturally, don't they, girls?

OMNES. Certainly!

[TAKE IN No. 5.]

(*during refrain the* GIRLS *walk mincingly round* GOBO, *who stands,* C., *horror-struck*)

GOBO. Well, I am ashamed of you. I don't believe poor little Lotos-Leaf would behave so, homeless wanderer though she is. And by-the-bye, where is she?

BABET. Where she should be—doing our work.

OMNES. Ha, ha, ha!

BABET. Yes, she's cutting faggots in the wood, and we girls go and gather flowers, which is less trouble.

GOBO. It's no affair of mine, so long as you are true to one who—(*horns off*) O dear, O dear! the Prince is coming!

OMNES. Is he! How is my back hair? (*duett for cornets— hunting refrain kept up till all are on*)

Enter HUNTSMEN, ASTRONOMER-ROYAL, GRAND MUDDLE *and* LAUREATE, *rapidly,* R.—*then* PRINCE LEO *followed by* FIDELIO, *to whom he hands gun—follow immediately next number.*

[TAKE IN No. 6.]

LEO. Ah, Gobo, straggler: we thought we had lost you. What sport—how many head of game?

GOBO. The royal hunt has not been unproductive. (*lets cat out of bag*) Behold! (ALL *laugh*)

LEO. But, my lords and friends, it was not sport alone led me here to-day. Guess, my counsellors, what it was?

ASTRON. Let me consult the stars. (*looks through theodolite—* GOBO *quietly puts up drinking flask in front*) Lunch. I see it distinctly.

MUDDLE. To confer with me on politics.

LAUR. To hear me recite my new poem, beginning:
  " Of man's first disobedience, and the seed
    Of that forbidden fruit, whose mortal taste——"
Shall I continue?

OMNES. (*forcibly*) No, no!

LEO. (*laughing*) Wrong—every one of you. (*to* PAGE) Tell them, Fidelio, of our adventure the other day and its result.

FIDEL. (*after bowing*) A week ago, the Prince, attended by myself, rode through a solitary bridle-path in yonder forest

On a sudden he stopped, and on following his glance, we saw a young woman——

LEO. An angel. (*clasping hands*)

FIDEL. (*hurt*) Your pardon, prince, a young woman.

LEO. No, a spirit, not of this earth.

FIDEL. Well, but angels don't carry faggots.

LEO. On this occasion one did.

FIDEL. She was not very short, (*all the sisters get on tiptoe*) nor yet very tall (*they all cower down*) She had a very pretty smile, (*they all grin diabolically*) and in fact was a very nice-looking girl.

THE SISTERS. (*coughing conceitedly*) H'm!

LEO. Profanity! Let me finish. She was a perfect being, an epitome of sweet perfection, and in a word—I love her!

OMNES. Ah!

ASTRON. (*aside to* LAUREATE) That is our secret enemy.

GOBO. (*aside*) My brain is in a whirl, let me reflect. (*business*)

BABET. (*aside*) I do remember being in the woods about then.

MUDDLE. Permit me, my gracious Prince, did you confide the fact of your sudden impression to the damsel—the—the— in fact the faggot-gathering angel?

LEO. No; (*sadly*) she vanished. I saw her no more.

LAUR. }
MUDDLE. } (*delighted*) Hurrah!
ASTRON. }

LEO. What?

ASTRON. She had returned to her native skies. Hence our joy.

LEO. Native fiddlesticks. I am certain she lives in this neighbourhood, and as there are not many houses, why——

BABET. (*curtseying*) There is only ours, please your mightiness.

LEO. Ha! A pretty girl.

GOBO. (*wildly*) No, no. Never!

BABET. Get along with you, sir. (*to* GOBO—*turning him behind her*)

LEO. But not my angel.

        (*all the* SISTERS *laugh*; BABETTE *retires, huffed*)

GOBO. No, she's not an angel. I told you you wouldn't do, Babette.

OTHER SISTERS. (*curtseying*) Please, your highness, we're the other inhabitants; we're not very short, and we're not very tall, we have a pretty smile, and we gather faggots. (*the* PRINCE *surveys them, and the* ASTRONOMER *theodolites them— business*)

LEO. No, you are very nice girls, but not she I seek. (*they retire abashed*) Are there no other girls about?

GOBO. None, these sisters are the lot. They live in yonder cottage.

LEO. Then must it have been a vision?

MUDDLE. Of course—an apparition. (*aside to others*) It's all right.

LEO. Therefore, gentlemen, to the hunt again!

OMNES. Bravo!

LEO. (*aside—advancing a pace*) I will return alone. Doubtless the crowd has scared her. (*aloud*) Gobo, to your post! Fidelio, my gun, and now, to the forest!

> (*réprise of the chorus only of the hunting song, which is repeated till all are off—the* PRINCE *and his following,* R., *and* BABETTE *and* SISTERS *into cottage by door*)

As soon as all are off, enter LOTOS-LEAF *timidly,* L., *carrying a large bundle of thorn sticks—she comes cautiously,* C., *and deposits her bundle.*

LOTOS. I thought I heard hunting horns—no one? So much the better, because old Huberlu doesn't like visitors; and when any come and annoy him, he expresses his sense of injury by beating me. I don't quite understand anything about it except the beating. That, I understand perfectly. Then his daughters say I ought to gather their faggots for them, and if I don't, they beat me too. They are a very able-bodied family. I sometimes think, after being beaten by Huberlu, because some one's toot-tooing on a horn in his vicinity, and after being jointly and severally beaten by his six daughters because I can't do all their work at once, I sometimes think life is a little monotonous. But I like night—for then I dream, oh! such dreams—of handsome princes who come and politely carry home my faggots for me, and then, and then, I awake and find I am only poor little Lotos-Leaf whom nobody owns!

[TAKE IN No. 7.]

Enter LEO, R., *on last bar—he starts on seeing her.*

LEO. (*aside*) Oh! my heart *was* right.

LOTOS. (*picking up sticks*) Now, I'd better get in, or old Huberlu will beat me. Ah, when will that handsome young Prince I dream of come and help me to carry my faggots?

LEO. (*advancing and taking sticks*) He is here! (*quickly*) Don't scream.

LOTOS. Please, sir, I wasn't going to.

LEO. (*putting faggots off at wing*) Quite self-possessed. (*returning*) So you are not *very* surprised, eh?

LOTOS. No; I have been dreaming about you some time.

LEO. And do dreams always come true?

LOTOS. If you remember them.
LEO. And you didn't forget me then ?
LOTOS. Oh, no !

[TAKE IN NO. 8.]

LEO. Do you think you could care for me ?
LOTOS. If you didn't beat me much.
LEO. Beat you !
LOTOS. I shouldn't mind it now and then, of course.
LEO. My dear ! by the way, what's your name ?
LOTOS. Lotos-Leaf.
LEO. Well, my dear Lotos-Leaf, to cut matters short, I am awfully infatuated with you, and I want to marry you.
LOTOS. Then why don't you ?
LEO. (*delighted*) Why don't I ? Now, there's charming simplicity for you ! But you dear little rustic, you, I must ask your pa and your ma.
LOTOS. Haven't got any pa or ma to speak of.
LEO. What about old what's-his-name ?
LOTOS. Huberlu ?
LEO. Exactly. Tooraloo.
LOTOS. Oh ! he's not my father. He's a very wicked old sorcerer.
LEO. Then, the sooner you're away the better. Come ! be my princess, and we will be married at once. Your *trousseau* will be ordered this day, and we'll spend our honeymoon at the court of my friend the Jewel King. What do you say ?
LOTOS. Oh, I am too happy to say anything !
LEO. Then let us sing it !

Enter FIDELIO *quickly*, R.

FIDEL. We await your highness ! (*aside*) The angel of the faggots !

[TAKE IN No. 8½.]

Exeunt R., LEO, LOTOS-LEAF, *and* FIDELIO—*stage dark — thunder and lightning.*

Enter HUBERLU *in his sorcerer's disguise*, L.—*he comes on frailly.*

HUBER. Aye—aye—aye—Age is beginning to tell on me. So I said to myself this morning, don't forget you were a sorcerer in your time, and know charms and specifics against old age. And I've been into the ravine, and have got some simples—a nice toad, and a newt, and a spotted snake, and other condiments—and I'll brew——

Enter SATANELLA, *suddenly*, R.

SATANEL. You're an old fool, and no conjuror.

HUBER. (*awed*) Hail, O Satanella!

SATANEL. When twenty years ago, you said you wished to retire from our active service, and marry and perpetuate your imbecile race, we granted your request.

HUBER. You did, O Queen.

SATANEL. But we told you that we might require your services again. So I brought you a child of Fate—Lotos-Leaf—and charged you by all that could awe you or control you, to watch over her safety, that never more should she leave the forest.

HUBER. You did.

SATANEL. And how have you discharged your trust?

HUBER. You shall see. (*calling*) Lotos-Leaf, Lotos-Leaf! (*pause*) Hither, you baggage, will you! Lotos-Leaf!

SATANEL. You may spare your lungs. She is gone.

HUBER. Gone?

SATANEL. Yes, with Prince Leo,—predestined to win her, and yet who would not—had I but chosen tools sharper than thee.

HUBER. What shall I do, great Satanella?

SATANEL. Find her.

HUBER. In this attire?

SATANEL. (*touching him with her wand*) No; you must seek her in palaces; be thyself a King. (HUBERLU'S *disguise goes, and he comes out as a grey-beard King. Lights up*) Be thine the task to separate Leo and Lotos-Leaf. So long as they are together I am powerless, and must call in mortal aid. Once separated, I will take care they shall never meet more.

HUBER. But my travelling state, my retinue?

SATANEL. True. You have daughters?

HUBER. Six.

SATANEL. Call them.

HUBER. Babette, Marotte, Berthe, Jacqueline; Ho! all of you.

(*the six little windows open simultaneously, and the six* SISTERS *put out their heads, still adorned with their peasants' caps*)

SATANEL. (*waving her wand*) Change! (*all the six caps disappear, giving place to boys' wigs*)

SISTERS. Oh, oh!

(*they shut windows simultaneously—put on pages' caps, and immediately troop out of door, and form in semi-circle round* HUBERLU, *as pages*)

HUBER. My daughters!

SATANEL. Your pages henceforth.

BABET. What will Gobo say!

HUBER. But where are the Prince and Princess gone?
(*during preceding speeches*, ELECTRA *has been worked up trap*, C., *and appears behind, just in time to take up cue*)

ELECT. To the Court of the Jewel King.

SATANEL. Then follow, and find them.

[TAKE IN No. 9.]

Exeunt SATANELLA, R.—HUBERLU *and* PAGES, L. *and* ELECTRA *by trap, all together.—change.*

SCENE FOURTH.—*Set of all; Palace of the Jewel King; throne and side chairs,* L. 2 E.

[TAKE IN No. 9½.]

March—Enter the JEWEL COURT, GUARDS, *&c.; lastly, the* QUEEN OF JEWELS—*she seats herself on throne—march stops.*

QUEEN. My faithful subjects! to-day, the anniversary of my wedding with the King of Jewels, is again arrived. He is at present out, but will not fail to be of our merriment. (*horns off*) Ha! What is that? Strangers?*

Enter DULCET, R. U. E.

[TAKE IN No. 10.]

Enter LEO *during Chorus, conducting* LOTOS-LEAF, *and followed by* FIDELIO *and* GOBO, *and the three* MINISTERS— *Chorus stops as they arrive opposite throne.*

LEO. Most gracious Queen, let me present to you my bride, the Princess Lotos-Leaf.

QUEEN. (*rising and embracing* LOTOS-LEAF) Fair Princess! I have read about your remarkable history in the papers. Be happy!

LOTOS. Madam, you overwhelm me!

QUEEN. My husband is out driving somewhere, but I expect him every minute.

LEO. No excuses, I beg; you of yourself are quite enough.

---

* The opening recitative of next number is to be sung all out of tune and time by a grotesque herald of the Jewel Court. At the conclusion, bouquets are to be thrown to him from four entrances (off), amid cries of "*Encore!*" He collects bouquets, bows profoundly, and begins recitative again; breaks down, and rushes off. The orchestra then pass straight to full chorus, and entrance of Prince Leo.

GOBO. (*aside*) I should think she was.

ASTRON. (*aside, to* LAUREATE) If Satanella means to do any-thing she'd better be quick about it.

MUDDLE. (*aside*) This will bring down my grey hairs in sorrow. (*wig business*)

LAUR. (*picking it up*) Sufficient for the day is the peruke thereof. (*trumpet call off*)

OMNES. Ha!

Enter DULCET, *announcing.*

DULCET. The King of the Source of the Nile and suite.

QUEEN. Admit him. *Exit* COURTIER. Source of the Nile!

LEO.
GOBO.
ASTRON. } Source of the Nile! (*separately, in different tones*
LAUR. *expressing perplexity*)
MUDDLE.

OMNES. (*together*) This is mysterious.

Enter, rapidly, R.U.E., HUBERLU *as King, followed by his six daughters as pages; they advance,* C., *and salaam to* QUEEN *together;* LEO *and* LOTOS *at* JEWEL QUEEN'S *side.*

HUBER. Being in your vicinity, O great Queen, it was my duty and my pleasure, as a brother potentate, to present myself before you.

QUEEN. I am delighted to see you.

HUBER. (*aside*) They are here. (*aloud*) Of course my name and title are well known to you?

QUEEN.
LEO.
GOBO. } Certainly! (*exactly in same tones as* " *Source*
ASTRON. *of the Nile*")
LAUR.
MUDDLE.

OMNES. Oh, certainly!

HUEBR. (*to* LEO) Prince, I knew your father, and let me congratulate his son on such a beautiful bride.

LOTOS. (*curtseying*) Oh, sire.

LEO. Shall we promenade? (*aside*) Don't like the look of that fellow!

(*gives arm to* LOTOS-LEAF—*they go slowly up stage— business—the* QUEEN *waves* FIDELIO *to her, he goes unwillingly—she takes his arm—they go up—meanwhile* GOBO *has been eyeing* BABETTE *with evident astonishment —the* PAGES *now go up arm-in-arm, two by two,* BABETTE *last—as she is passing* GOBO *he arrests her attention*)

GOBO. Eh!—what—never—Bab——

BABET. Fellow!

GOBO. I beg your pardon.

BABET. Ha, ha, ha! (*goes up*)

GOBO. (*scratching plume*) Let me reflect. (*goes up reflecting—almost simultaneously* HUBERLU *has crossed to three* MINISTERS *and laid his finger on lip*)

HUBER. ⎫
ASTRON. ⎬ Hist!
LAUR. ⎭
MUDDLE. ⎭

HUBER. The word!

ASTRON. I will letter or halve it with you.

HUBER. Sat—

ASTRON. An—

LAUR. Ell—

MUDDLE. A!

    (ALL *wink simultaneously—slap right hand on closed mouth, then clap hands together—turn round on left leg, crack fingers and strike attitude*)

HUBER. 'Tis deeply sworn!

Enter DULCET, *announcing*, R. U. E.

DULCET. The Jewel King!

OMNES. Ah!   (*next number quick—picture for entrance*)

[TAKE IN No. 11.]

Enter JEWEL GUARDS—*then* JEWEL KING *on velocipede with* OUTRIDERS, *&c. —gets down, embraces his* QUEEN, *and salutes his* VISITORS—*the velocipede wheels off, all to the music of chorus, and rapidly.*

OMNES. Long live the Jewel King!

KING. Nonsense, nonsense, my good friends; your sentiments do you more credit than your wisdom. How can a potentate of my dimensions live *long?* (*to* LEO) And so you are about to perpetrate matrimony, prince?

LEO. This be my excuse. (*pointing to* LOTOS-LEAF)

KING. A very charming one. (*looking at* LOTOS-LEAF *through eye-glass*) What do you weigh, my dear?

LOTOS. I—I—really don't know, your majesty.

KING. Ah! that's a pity. I like a fine woman. My wife is a fine woman. What do you think of her, Leo?

LEO. Seldom have I seen so much beauty—all at once!

KING. Right. Eh, my poppet. (*tries to kiss her and fails*)

QUEEN. (*confused*) Don't, I am but a feeble woman. (*to* LOTOS-LEAF) Won't you come, my dear, and select your own rooms, for you'll stay with us I hope some time.

LOTOS. With pleasure.

Goes up with QUEEN, *followed by* FIDELIO, *and exit,* L. U. E.

HUBER. (*aside*) Now for it. (*pantomimic business for him and three* MINISTERS *exactly as before*)

LEO. (*who has gone up and blown kisses off—returning*) Ah, how graceful she looks as she disappears from sight.

KING. That's one advantage my wife possesses over other women—she never disappears from sight.

HUBER. She is indeed a splendid figure.

KING. Sir, one figure couldn't express her. Ah! when one meets a woman like that, matrimony is a beautiful institution——

GOBO. To keep clear of.

KING. Eh?

LEO. Silence, Gobo!

BABET. (*forgetting herself*) Oh you wretch!

GOBO. What! eh? Bab——

BABET. (*remembering*) Fellow!

GOBO. I beg your pardon, sir. (*scratching head*) Let me reflect.

LEO. My poet laureate has always tried to dissuade me from love.

KING. Has he?

LAUR. (*advancing*) On the contrary—my verses recommend to all lovers the example of the butterfly, which woos every flower but is constant to none.

LEO. Isn't that a dreadful sentiment.

KING. It's well the ladies are gone. (*pokes* LEO *in ribs*)

LAUR. (*producing music*) I have a little song here on the subject.

KING. (*taking it*) Ourself shall try it.

OMNES. Bravo!

[TAKE IN No. 12.]

(*During the chorus, a dancing movement without stirring from places*)

Enter DULCET, L. U. E.

DULCET. May it please your Majesty, the guards of the household await your Majesty's pleasure.

KING. Let them enter.   *Exit* TRUMPETER, L. U. E.
(*to* LEO) A little parade I offer you. Will you be seated, Prince. (*to* HUBERLU) Brother, this way.

(*they take their places at side.*)

[GRAND BALLET.]

(*Ballet over—*QUEEN *shrieks off, then rushes on, followed by* FIDELIO—*picture of astonishment—the* QUEEN *faints, and*

is recovered by KING—*meanwhile,* FIDELIO *comes down,*
C. *front, and principals close round in semi-circular lines*
for dialogue—all to be done simultaneously, and rapidly)

LEO. What's wrong? Speak! Where is the Princess Lotos-Leaf?

FIDEL. Gone.

OMNES. Gone?

LEO. But where? Speak—speak!

FIDEL. Alas, I know not.

QUEEN. She vanished from my side as if by magic, and much I fear she is in the power of some wicked fairy.

HUBER. (*aside*) Satanella!

LEO. If it be so, then I have a counter-charm. My godmother, Snowflake, promised at my baptism that she would guard me against the Evil Eye, and against every spell. What I never sought for myself, I now invoke for my lost love.

[TAKE IN No. 13.]

The Fairy SNOWFLAKE *appears on last bars—picture to receive*
her.

SNOW. Fear nothing, O Prince, for you will recover her you love, although the arts of my rival, Satanella, will prevail for the moment. Many dangers Lotos-Leaf will pass through, and many lands must you visit in your search; but love on, trust on, and you will conquer in the end. (*a white* DOVE *rises from stage and wings up to flies*) Lo! the sign and emblem of the first spell cast on her you love. Seek Lotos-Leaf in the far kingdom of the birds!

ELECTRA *has risen up through trap close to* HUBERLU.

ELECT. (*aside to* HUBERLU) To Japan! where lies the way to the bird land. They must be stopped there!

KING. Courage! Prince. (*aside—shaking his hand*) I'll go with you, but don't tell my wife!

LEO. Lotos-Leaf! my Lotos-Leaf.

[TAKE IN No. 14.]

(*final picture on last movement of finale*— SATANELLA
appears at back in dragon chariot with LOTOS-LEAF
suppliant at her feet—LEO *tries to go to her but is held*
back by HUBERLU *and* PAGES—ELECTRA, R., *as Spirit of*
Mischief—SNOWFLAKE, L. C.—*the rest in groups pointing*
to SATANELLA—*curtain, slow*)

END OF THE FIRST ACT.

Characters in Second Act.

THE TYCOON (*Huberlu*) ... ...

HIS SIX PAGES (*Babette and Sisters*)

LEO (*travelling as Oriental Prince*) ...

THE ASTRONOMER-ROYAL ...

THE POET LAUREATE ... ...

THE HEREDITARY GRAND MUDDLE

SATANELLA ... ...

SNOWFLAKE (*in disguise mantle*) ...

ELECTRA ... ...

FIDELIO ... ...

GOBO ... ...

KING JEWEL ... ...

EMPEROR EAGLE ... ...

LOTOS-LEAF (*as the Lone Dove*) ...

Japanese Crowd—amongst whom four Bastinado Men and Palanquin Bearers.   The Empire of Birds.   Court of the Bird Emperor.

GRAND PLUMED BALLET.

ACT II.

Mysterious Storm Music to raise curtain; Stage discovered empty; rain and wind. Enter, rapidly, to the music, under umbrellas, R.U.E., *the* ASTRONOMER, LAUREATE *and* MUDDLE; *they bear carpet bags and other travelling gear.*

MUDDLE. When Prince Leo announced his intention of travelling to Japan, I did not anticipate that his Cabinet was to accompany him; much less that his ministers of state were to act as agents in advance. Where are we?

ASTRON. (*theodolitizing*) Can't say; no stars visible—and if there were they would be foreigners and I couldn't understand them. (*rain and wind*) Ugh! pleasant weather. (*wig business*)

LAUR. I have just composed a poem on it. (*producing paper and reading*)

> " The day is cold, and dark, and dreary,
> It rains, and the wind is never weary;
> Yet the vine still clings to the mouldering wall—
> Though at every gust the dead leaves fall."

And the day, my friends, is pretty considerably dark and dreary.

(*the* ASTRONOMER *and* MUDDLE *are much affected, and bury their heads,* R. *and* L., *in handkerchiefs*)

ASTRON. } No more! No more!
MUDDLE. }

LAUR. (*eagerly*) Listen! Next verse shows that something must turn up.

(*meanwhile* ELECTRA *has been worked quietly up trap behind* LAUREATE—*she leans on his shoulder, and takes up cue quickly*)

ELECT. My dear Laureate, something *has* turned up.

OMNES. Electra! (*chord ff.*)

ELECT. So don't read any more of your verses.

LAUR. (*aside*) Just my luck. 1 never get beyond the first stanza.

ELECT. I bear great news.

MUDDLE. If you'd bear great coats, it would be to the purpose.

ASTRON. The humidity is excessive.

ELECT. You are right. (*waving arm*) Geni! a little less rain, please, and reserve your darkness for your victims. (*lights up—wind ceases*)

THE THREE MINISTERS. That is much better.

ELECT. (*to* GENI) Thanks, Geni. (*to* MINISTERS, *bringing them down*) Gentlemen, your travels are over!

THE THREE. O joy! Likewise, O rapture! (*sung*)

ELECT. You are surprised?

MUDDLE. Hem! O dear, no! I always thought my diplomatic talents would bring the affair through.

ELECT. Nonsense. The same power that directs all statesmanship has been your best help here.

MUDDLE. And that is——?

ELECT. Chance!

MUDDLE. I don't remember any statesman of that name.

ELECT. Very likely not. But Chance has led you and the Prince hither—to the dread valley of the Fateful Cliffs. Against the life of Leo and Lotos-Leaf we are powerless; neither Satanella nor myself can work them that harm. But Chance has led the Prince into an enchanter's land—one of our most powerful geni—who has the charm of life and death. He will end this romantic Prince, and so cut the knot of your perplexities. Leo is doomed!

ASTRON. So his horoscope said. I couldn't make out exactly what it meant when I cast it, but I now see plainly what it referred to.

LAUR. (*with emotion*) Perhaps it would be a comfort for the Prince to know that I will write an elegy on him. I have just thought of a little trifle beginning—"Not a drum was heard, not a funeral note."

ELECT. That'll do.

LAUR. (*bitterly*) As usual!

ELECT. The Prince is at hand!

ASTRON. Within a few minutes of us, his avant-couriers.

ELECT. Then away! Lest you too be involved in his destruction.

MUDDLE. O by all means; let's be off.

ASTRON. But whither?

ELECT. To the City of the Daimios. There Satanella awaits intelligence. Huberlu also. You will rejoice them greatly, and add to your own importance.

MUDDLE. I will prepare a state paper upon it.

ELECT. (*laughing*) And give all the credit to the wrong

people! Now farewell. I go to report progress to Plutus.

*Trap music—*ELECTRA *sinks—for a moment the three* MINISTERS *stand perplexed by trap, when a terrific roll of thunder makes them start—lightning, wind and rain, and Storm Music as before—business of opening umbrellas and comic exit* L. 2 E.*—lights down from* ELECTRA'S *exit— the wind and rain kept up softly all through scene till end, with occasional roll of distant thunder.*

Enter R. 2 E. SNOWFLAKE *disguised as old peasant with rough pole, and apparently guiding on* LEO, FIDELIO, GOBO *and* JEWEL KING, *who enter all in strip fugitive dresses; Orchestra goes straight on with symphony of next number.*

[TAKE IN No. 15.]

KING. Well, Prince, if I had thought this love chase of yours would have led us into such a place as this, I think I would have stayed at home. (*with emotion*) Ah! my wife should have been a law unto me.

GOBO. Law? Yes, the statutes at large!

LEO. Silence, knave! My dear King, we must be near somewhere; besides our faithful ministers are sure to clear the way for us. Are we on the trail?

FIDEL. (*picking up paper*) Yes, here is a MS. poem by the Laureate. Shall I read it?

OMNES. No, no!

LEO. Ah, Lotos-Leaf, where art thou?

GOBO. Ah, Babette!

KING. (*to* LEO, *aside*) Do you think our guide is all right, eh?

LEO. (*aside to him*) I'll see. (*to* SNOWFLAKE) Old man, we have trusted you to guide us to the City of the Daimios, and methinks this is a strange way to it. Where are we?

SNOW. In the enchanted valley of an evil Geni, whose thunders even now threaten you!

GOBO. Oh dear, oh dear! I want to go home.

LEO. And you lead us into this peril?

SNOW. It was willed so by fate. (*strain of duett, First Act*) You love this Princess, truly then?

LEO. Ah! I can love her memory even; then how much more her living, breathing self—if such there be!

SNOW. (C.) Then, fear nothing—for here, as in the deepest pit of the nether world, love rules and reigns without a rival power. Even here the Geni must **bow** before pure love.

(*Music stops—demon laughter off*)

OMNES. Ah!

LEO. That demon laughter—thy warning words—this gloomy solitude, what means it all?

DEEP VOICE. (*off*) Death!

> (*Music increases—thunder and lightning—three distinct crashes in orchestra—at the third, a general exclamation of horror—the cliffs fall forward—change—Music stops suddenly*)

SCENE SECOND.—*Market Place in the City of the Daimios, Japan—lights up.*

White lime-lights on stage, which is discovered empty, except the principals of end of last Scene, now in rich dresses; LEO recognises SNOWFLAKE.

LEO. My kind fairy!

SNOW. Love on, hope on.

LEO. But where are we?

SNOW. In the City of the Daimios; and see the populace come. (*symphony of next number pp. in orchestra*) I must away. Beware of false friends—and on to the Empire of the Birds. Farewell! *Exit*, L. 1 E.

GOBO. O, what a funny lot of people! (*looking off*, R.)

Enter from upper entrances, R. and L., the JAPANESE POPULACE, *singing next Chorus, during this they parade stage with fruit-baskets, fish, birds, feathers for sale, &c., and on final bars group under umbrellas, and at stalls, &c., the principals standing watching them,* L. 1 E.

[TAKE IN No. 16.]

Upon last bars of Chorus, enter in palanquin HUBERLU *as Tycoon, surrounded by* BABETTE *and* SISTERS, *as Japanese Pages—they come, C.—*HUBERLU *descends, and the palanquin and bearers go up and remain in picture at back—all the* JAPANESE POPULACE *prostrate themselves on stage as the Tycoon descends, then rise and form new semi-circular tableau—all this in the music—dialogue to proceed the moment the music stops.*

HUBER. We, the Tycoon of Japan—(*chord*) cousin of the moon—(*chord*) and uncle of the sun—(*chord*) having heard that strangers had dared to penetrate to our capital, demand of them their designations, and their business.

LEO. Great luminary, I am Prince Leo of Gaul, travelling

with these my friends and escort, in search of my lost bride, the Princess Lotos-Leaf.

KING. And I, King Jewel, have left *my* wife, to assist my friend in finding *his.*

GOBO. And I, Gobo, seeing no prospect of ever getting back to Babette, am also looking for an eligible girl.

BAB. (*forgetting herself*) Wretch! (*hits him over the head with her fan*)

GOBO. Oh! (*from that time looks astonished at* BABETTE)

HUBER. Welcome, noble strangers! And where may the Princess be?

LEO. In the Empire of the Birds.

HUBER. Ah! in the domains of the plumed Emperor, a neighbouring potentate. Between ourselves rather a volatile monarch—very flighty.

LEO. (*uneasy*) But you don't think——eh?

HUBER. No, no, no—'Tis a long way from here, Prince, and your retinue is small!

KING. Alas! our poor Laureate (*handkerchief*)

FIDEL. That dear Astronomer! (*handkerchief*)

GOBO. My own Muddle! (*handkerchief*)

LEO. Lost—devoted servants—(*handkerchief*)

HUBER. Dear me! this is very sad. But we will try to make it up to you. (*aside*) I must detain him for Satanella. (*aloud*) You will stay with us a week or two.—You need repose—and the way is perilous.

LEO. Your luminary is indeed kind.

FIDEL. (*aside to* LEO) Remember Snowflake's advice—trust no stranger.

LEO. (*aside to him*) Ha, I had forgotten! (*aloud to* HUBERLU) My faithful page reminds me that our duty points onward. No, luminary, I must decline your hospitality.

HUBER. (*aside*) Confusion! (*aloud*) At least you will eat and drink with me? Lo, my palace! (*pointing off,* R.) Come, all is prepared.

GOBO. Certainly—we accept!

LEO. Silence, sirrah! Luminary, I am at your service!

[TAKE IN No. 17.]

On last bars the palanquin is brought down, but HUBERLU *motions it away—they take it off,* R. 2 E.—HUBERLU *gives hand to* LEO, *the others form in twos, and the Royal Procession goes off to music,* R., *except* GOBO *and* BABETTE, *who remain looking at each other—business—simultaneously the* POPULACE *form and go off,* L., *singing—stage clear for* GOBO *and* BABETTE—*they break up and come* C., *front.*

27

GOBO. (*aside*) He reminds me amazingly of Babette.

BABET. (*aside*) There's that poor dear Gobo, and I mustn't tell him!

GOBO. (*aside*) Should like to embrace him for Babette.

BABET. (*aside*) O for one good hug!

GOBO. H'm!

BABET. H'm! Why don't you go in with the rest?

GOBO. Why don't you?

BABET. (*pretending to sob*) Because my love is far away!

GOBO. (*overcome*) So is mine!

BABET. Eating is out of the question.

GOBO. Sympathy is what *I* want.

BABET. Poor young man!

GOBO. Dear boy! (*they embrace*)

BABET. (*aside*) I feel better!

GOBO. (*aside*) Now that's very odd. First of all I meet a page in the Jewel Court, and I think it is Babette; now I come across a Jap, and, lo! I think it is Babette again. Let me reflect. (*business*) Can't make it out. (*suddenly*) Let's sympathize again.

BABET. Come on! (*they embrace*) And now luncheon.

GOBO. Well, I feel like eating now.

> *They exeunt,* R.—*Music in orchestra,* " *See the Conquering Hero comes.*"

Enter abreast, L. U. E., *arm in arm, and lifting legs pompously,* LAUREATE, ASTRONOMER, *and* MUDDLE—*they come down, and music stops.*

ASTRON. (*theodolitizing*) This is the place. From solar observation, I perceive we are near Satanella and Huberlu.

MUDDLE. This time we can hold our own. What news for her! (*producing roll*) Here is an abstract for the archives of Plutus of our labours. I will read it her.

LAUR. No you won't. (*producing paper*) On such occasions the Muse of Poetry steps in. I have composed an epic of one thousand three hundred cantos on the subject. Hem! I begin thus—

> Hope, for a season, bade the world farewell,
> And Freedom shrieked when young Prince Leo fell—
> At least she would have shrieked, had not the Laureate
> Remarked there wasn't anything to be sorry at.

Shall I continue?

THE OTHERS. (*vehemently*) No, no!

ASTRON. For my part, I think your written addresses are cold and formal. Now I was thinking, that if I give a little off-hand speech, alluding to the clever way in which I managed the expedition. (*they commence to wrangle,* L. 1 E., *speaking together in an undertone*)

28

LAUR. } Well, I can't see that. My poem—I insist on it —I——

MUDDLE. } She must hear my stale papers. Excuse me, gentlemen, but——

ASTRON. } Yes, my view is correct—no use arguing—I shall do it. (*this is kept up*)

Enter SATANELLA *followed by* HUBERLU, R.,—*she is angry and speaks coming on.*

SATANEL. Am I never to triumph? Those idiots of ministers first, then you. If, as you say, you cannot retain Leo here, follow him to the Empire of Birds. Away!

HUBERLU *salaams and exit,* R.

(*she comes down—the* MINISTERS *turn as she speaks next sentence*) So you are here?

THE THREE. Satanella! (*chord*)

(*they all get on their knees, backs to public, and salute, Oriental fashion, by touching stage with forehead*)

THE THREE. (*raising heads*) We have come for our reward!

SATANEL. And you shall have it. (*waves wand off*)

THE THREE. Thanks, great Satanella!

SATANEL. I know my service is nearest your hearts.

THE THREE. It is! On our souls be it. (*they bow again*)

Enter two JAPANESE *with long bamboo, and two more with canes.*

SATANEL. It *shall* be on your soles!

(*motions to* ATTENDANT—*the two* BAMBOO MEN *run their pole under the insteps of the three, and raise soles in air—the rest cane them unmercifully, while the* MINISTERS *roar for mercy*)

SATANEL. Enough! (*the* JAPANESE *go off,* R.) Remember my arm is long, and I am not to be trifled with! *Exit,* L.

(*the three, with a groan, roll over on their backs, and lie* C. *of stage—First Chorus of Scene repeated to bring on all the crowd as before—then* PAGES, *then* HUBERLU, LEO, GOBO, *and* FIDELIO)

GOBO. (*tripping against* MINISTERS) Hallo! three gentlemen rooming out!

HUBER. Dogs! Throw them into the river!

(*the* MINISTERS *sit up back to back with alacrity*)

THE THREE. No! no!

LEO. What! my ministers!

OMNES. Ah!

LEO. How come you in this plight? But I see, faithful friends, it is in my service you have suffered.

ASTRON. Yes, indeed!

29

HUBER. I can see you are foot-sore!

LAUR. Oh, we are!

GOBO. You have come through a deal of cane?

MUDDLE Yes, that we have.

LEO. Well, rise—and rejoice with me. We are now on the confines of the Bird Kingdom. Lotos-leaf shall be mine!

HUBER. (aside) Perhaps! (the three rise and limp)

THE THREE. (aside) Vengeance on Lotos-leaf! (wig business)

FIDEL. (to GOBO) These fellows are traitors.

GOBO. Of course; but it don't signify.

HUBER. Then Prince, if you are bent on this expedition, I will go too.

KING. You are a good fellow, Tycoon!

BABET. (aside) Oh! is he—vous verrez, mon petit bon homme! (picture for finale)

[TAKE IN No. 18.]

SCENE THIRD.—A Suburb of Twitterville, capital of the Bird Empire; cloth in 1st; tropical wood scene, with all kinds of gaily plumaged birds painted among the foliage.

Characteristic Music to express each class of comic birds, and enter the COURT of the Bird Emperor, R. and L., separately; the OWLS with spectacles, and bearing MSS. rolls under their wings; the STORKS with halberds; the CROWS as parsons, with white bands; the PARROTS with Congress tickets on them ("Congressman from Indiana," &c."); when all are on and in picture, enter EMPEROR EAGLE, attended by COCK ROBIN as Court Barber, and JENNY WREN as Mistress of the Robes; "Hail Columbia" to bring EAGLE on; he is thoughtful, and rubs his beak reflectively.

EAGLE. Attendant fowls, and dear poultry, I am fain to consult with you to-day respecting myself. You must have observed a change in me lately?

OMNES. We have, great Eagle.

EAGLE. Yes; it is patent to every one.

JENNY. It struck me the other day your Majesty was moulting.

EAGLE. So I am, dear Miss Wren.

ROBIN. When I dressed your Majesty's hair this morning, it struck me that the imperial head was even balder than usual.

EAGLE. It is; I fear I must take to night-caps. Now, what is it that thus disturbs me, and disarranges my system? (to CROWS) My dear parsons, can you give me any notion?

30

1st Crow. It is because your Majesty hasn't been regular to meeting lately.

Eagle (*to* Owls) And you, philosophers, what do you say?

1st Owl. The decrees of philosophy must not lightly be spoken. Therefore we must entreat your Majesty to allow us at least one century for deliberation.

Eagle. It is reasonable. (*to* Parrots) Well, gentlemen of Congress, what is the matter with your Eagle?

1st Parrot. Guess he ain't very sick after all? The air of France ain't good for your Majesty, but here out West you'll spread yourself, sure.

Eagle. (*smiling and shaking head*) Ah! my good friends, my malady is not a political nor yet a physical one. It is mental, it is here—(*beating heart*) beneath these quills. Yes, subject poultry, your Emperor loves!

Omnes. (*flapping wings and whistling*) Never!

Eagle. Yes—it is true. My old enjoyments pall upon my taste. To descend upon the sportive lamb and raise him up for dinner, delights me no more.

All. (*affected*) Alas!

Eagle. I used to revel in spread-eagleism in patriotic speeches. That, likewise, is played out.

All. Dear me.

Eagle. I was a flaunting fowl formerly, but I am now of a reflective and morbid tendency. I am thinking of devoting the remainder of life to improving my mind, and living in Boston.

All. No, no.

Eagle. You see my love is unrequited. That's the trouble.

1st Crow. But who is the haughty bird?

(Rooster *crows off*)

Eagle. My herald! Who comes!

Enter Rooster, R.—*he crows.*

Rooster. The White Dove craves an audience of the great Eagle.

Eagle. (*aside*) 'Tis she! (*aloud*) Let her hop in!

Rooster *crows and exits*, R.

The beautiful stranger Dove that has come amongst us.

Jenny. She gives herself airs.

1st Stork. Won't speak even to the upper classes.

1st Crow. This damsel is a snare.

Eagle. Hold your tongues, all of you, or I'll peck you.

Music—symphony of next number—enter Lotos-Leaf, *as the White Dove—she is pensive, pays no heed to anyone, and comes* c. *for her song.*

[TAKE IN No. 19.]

31

EAGLE. (*aside to* COURT) Noble poultry, take yourselves off. We would be alone.

> *Exeunt all,* R. *and* L., *except* LOTOS-LEAF *and* EAGLE— EAGLE *comes down and tries to embrace her—she repulses him.*

LOTOS. No liberties, you ugly wretch, you!

EAGLE. My dear Dove—you the type of gentleness! Now, had you been a young Eagle, or even one of my cousins the Vultures, I could have understood it; but you, a Dove—it is dreadful!

LOTOS. I'm not a Dove! I never wanted to be one: although I did sing at school, "I would I were a bird." But then I didn't know what a horrid existence it is.

EAGLE. (*shocked*) My dear!

LOTOS. Feathers are a mistake, and then to have to peck your food, and keep dabbing one's nose against the viands; not to mention sleeping on a branch at night, with one leg up, and my head under my left arm. It really is most uncomfortable! (*crosses*)

EAGLE. (*aside*) Poor young Dove. (*tapping forehead*) Always imagining she's somebody else. (*aloud—bringing her,* C.) Come, come, my dear, listen to me.

LOTOS. Well!

EAGLE. (*tenderly*) Have you never remarked anything peculiar about me?

LOTOS. Yes.

EAGLE. (*overjoyed*) Ah!

LOTOS. That you were the ugliest brute I ever saw out of a menagerie.

EAGLE. You joke!

LOTOS. O, dear, no. Quite serious.

EAGLE. And yet I love you.

LOTOS. (C.) Ridiculous!

EAGLE. (*kneeling* L. C. *of* LOTOS.) Yes! hear my suit. The Eagle Monarch is feeble before you!

Enter ROOSTER, R.—*he looks astonished, and stops when about to crow.*

I would not have my subjects know my weakness. And yet I love you madly—I adore you—I—(*sees* ROOSTER) Hallo! (*gets up rapidly*) D—n it, sir, why didn't you crow? (ROOSTER *crows energetically*) What is it now, eh?

ROOSTER. The Tycoon, your Majesty, and suite.

EAGLE. Show 'em in. (ROOSTER *crosses and exits,* R.) At such a moment too! Annoying!

LOTOS. Oh, please may I stay and see the strangers?

EAGLE. Certainly not. Retire to your perch.

32

LOTOS. (*going slowly*, L.) Can it be real—or is it a dream? Did my Leo really live? And if so, has he forgotten me! I am so unhappy. *Exits* L.

EAGLE. The Tycoon! What does he want, I wonder? I dont like these featherless bipeds; but I suppose one must be civil, even to the lower orders of creatures.

Enter BABETTE *and* PAGES *and range,* HUBERLU *leading* LEO, *and followed by* GOBO, FIDELIO, *and* THREE MINISTERS —*Picture.*

HUBER. Great Eagle, our brother, Prince Leo, of Gaul, having lost his Princess Lotos-Leaf, believes her to be in your dominions. I have in vain reasoned against this foolish belief. On your kingly word, the Princess——is she here or no?

EAGLE. I have no such person in all my realm.

LEO. O say not so. I *know* she is!

EAGLE. Has she wings? (LEO *shakes head*) Does she peck? Can she hop? No! well, she is not here.

THE THREE MINISTERS. Of course she's not.

LEO. (*to* FIDELIO) Who am I to believe, Fidelio?

FIDEL. Snowflake!

LEO. Right, and she it was who told me my love was here.

EAGLE. Well, you have the run of my dominions; go, seek every dwelling, if that alone will satisfy you.

LEO. O thanks, noble fowl! Come, Gobo.

GOBO. O I daresay. Are you aware, my Prince, where we'd have to go? Up trees, out branches, into nests, no, I don't quite see that. I think we'll take the Emperor's word for it.

LEO. Are your subjects then all birds? (*sounds of next number off*)

EAGLE. All. And as I'm a monarch, here is a little wedding party coming. Search for your princsss, if you like among their ranks.

Procession Music.—*Enter* CANARY BIRD MARRIAGE PRO-CESSION, R.,—*business—they exeunt.*

EAGLE. Well?

LEO. (*sobbing*) Alas! I fear I have lost her!

EAGLE. Come—come, don't give way like that! (*lowering his voice*) I know how you must feel, for I have been unfortunate in love myself.

LEO. (*interested*) Indeed.

EAGLE. Hush! speak low; love is weakness, and we kings mustn't confess to it. Yes, Prince, I love——

LEO. Who?

EAGLE. A Dove.

LEO. (*interested*) A Dove? (*strain of duett, First Act*)

33

EAGLE. Yes, a White Dove; she came lately to my kingdom, and we naturalized her quick, so as to vote at the next election.

LEO. And she returns your love?

EAGLE. No. But then she is mad.

LEO. Mad?

EAGLE. Yes; imagines herself a biped without feathers—a mere mortal like yourself.

LEO. Ha!

EAGLE. Says she has been enchanted. That she was a princess—mere lunacy in fact. Ha! ha!

LEO. (*aside*) A princess. (*aloud*) Emperor, I think I can cure this silly Dove.

EAGLE. You can? Then you shall. (*calling*) Ho, guards!

LEO. (*stopping him*) No, no! not before all those people! (*aside*) If it should be she? (*Music stops*)

EAGLE. Ah! you are right. (*to* OTHERS) I would speak with my brother of Gaul an instant. Affairs of state.

HUBER. (*aside*) I don't like the look of things.

FIDEL. (*aside*) Can he have found anything out?

BABET. I don't fancy this foreign land business.

GOBO. Then let us go and sympathize with each other.

ASTRON. (*to two* MINISTERS) Let us watch!

[TAKE IN No. 20.]

Exeunt all, R., *leaving* EAGLE *and* LEO.

EAGLE. And now to fetch her!   *Exit,* L.

LEO. (*rapturously*) Oh! if it should be her I love! Keep still my heart: she comes!

Enter EAGLE EMPEROR, L., *leading on* LOTOS-LEAF, *who keeps her eyes down, and never perceives* LEO.*

LEO. (*aside*) 'Tis she!

EAGLE. I have brought you, O White Dove, a stranger, who knows such maladies as yours, and will cure you of your silly fancies. (*incredulity of* LOTOS) Listen to him. (*to* LEO) Put forth your power.

[TAKE IN No. 21.]

(*during Duett,* LOTOS-LEAF *awakes to the consciousness that it is* LEO *who sings, and expresses her joy and love for him; all which the* EAGLE EMPEROR *believes intended for him*)

---

* LEO.   EAGLE.   LOTOS-LEAF.

L.

34

EAGLE. Marvellous! This is indeed a change. You are happier now, Dove?

LOTOS. Ever so much!

LEO. But the cure is not complete.

EAGLE. No!

LEO. One spell must yet be removed—and for that I must be left alone with her.

EAGLE. Certainly, dear Prince. Adieu, dear Dove, but not for long. *(going* L.) I will go, and in the exuberance of my joy, catch a few lambs for luncheon. *Goes off*, L.

LEO. Lotos-Leaf!

LOTOS. My Prince! *(they embrace—the heads of three* MINISTERS *appear at* R. *wing)*

LEO. Not a moment is to be lost—you must fly!

LOTOS. That I can do literally.

LEO. Fear not! The moment you leave the Empire of Birds you will be restored to your proper shape. We must not go together,—'twould excite suspicion and be fatal; therefore we must be yet apart, but for a little moment. Wait for me by the Grove of Palms, on the Argent river. Then love and happiness shall be ours.

> *Reprise of last ensemble of Duett—and exit* LOTOS-LEAF, R., LEO *blows kisses, then exit*, L., *all in the music—the moment he is off, lights down—and enter* ASTRONOMER, LAUREATE *and* MUDDLE.

ASTRON. Confusion.

LAUR. All is lost now—Ah, for ever, my——

MUDDLE. *(interrupting)* Plutus will cashier us.

OMNES. What is to be done?

Gong—SATANELLA *appears—lime-light on her*, R. C., *in vampyre in cloth—picture.*

SATANEL. *(giving cross-bow to* MUDDLE) Lotos-Leaf must not escape—shoot her.

MUDDLE. What! kill her?

SATANEL. No—that is impossible—but it will change the spell, and her form, and so again she will slip from the grasp of her lover.

ASTRON. There is no other means? *(trembles)*

LAUR. No way but that?

SATANEL. None, and let it be done quickly. See! she plumes herself for flight. Be warned, and for the last time!

> *Gong— Exit* SATANELLA—*vampyre closes.*

MUDDLE. I—I—I never was much of a shot. You try!

LAUR. No, I can only draw the long bow. Ask the Astronomer?

35

ASTRON. No: (*theodolite*) but I'll sight her for you!

(*business*—MUDDLE *places himself opposite entrance,* R., *and* LAUREATE *and* ASTRONOMER *tail on—he shoots—shriek off, and they all stagger back*)

Enter LEO, *quickly.*

LEO. What means that cry?

Chord—SNOW-FLAKE *appears in vampyre* L. C. *in cloth— lime-light.*

SNOW. It means that you must seek Lotos-leaf, not here— but in the stars. These miscreant minions of your foe Plutus, have, by a fatal arrow, changed her form, though they could not take her life.

LEO. Wretches! Murderers! (*they go on their knees*)

THE THREE. Pity! Mercy! Quarter!

LEO. (*threatening them with sword*) What mercy did you shew to her? You shall die!

SNOW. No; for their life shall be a punishment to them, and of service to you. I know that Lotos-Leaf's new home is in the stars, but which, I know not. Theirs be the task to find out where. When men are asleep, be theirs the punishment to read the glittering hieroglyphs of heaven, and to discover there the home of Lotos-Leaf.

THE THREE. (*groaning*) Oh—oh!

SNOW. As for you, Prince, be not cast down. The power of your foes is drawing to an end. Earth refuses to aid them longer, and now the exile of your love to a distant planet is the last transmigration possible. Love can scale the empyrean; and I say to you, fear not, but love on, purely and fondly, and Lotos-Leaf shall be restored to you. Meanwhile, you are yet in peril. The Eagle Emperor must know nought of this, or your life might be the forfeit. Be wary—dress your face in smiles—share in the revelries of the birds, then away once more! on the starry trail of your lost love. Farewell!

Exit SNOWFLAKE—*vampyre closes*—LEO *makes a step towards her, as if to retain her—the* MINISTERS *rise—lights up.*

LEO. One moment——

Music.—Re-enter R. *and* L., BIRD-GUARDS, HUBERLU *and* PAGES, FIDELIO, GOBO, ROBIN *and* WREN, EAGLE, &c.,— *Picture for finale.*

EAGLE. (*to* LEO) Where is my Dove—is the charm removed?

LEO. Almost, your majesty. She has gone to her nest, where she must remain undisturbed for two days—at the end of that time you will have a surprise.

EAGLE. (*shaking him by hand*) Now this *is* kind!

36

ELECTRA *rises behind* HUBERLU *by trap.*

ELECT. (*aside to* HUBERLU) Where is Lotos-Leaf?

HUBER. (*aside to him*) Dead?

ELECT. Nothing of the kind. She is translated.

HUBER. Whither?

ELECT. To Venus.

HUBER. Well?

ELECT. Follow her!

EAGLE. And now, noble friends, I invite you to a dance, or should I say a hop? We plume ourselves upon our accomplishments that way; and, I flatter myself, you will not regret having come to see the Emperor Eagle at his Birdcage Palace.

OMNES. (*clapping hands*) Bravo!

[TAKE IN No. 22]

Exeunt OMNES, *and change.*

SCENE FOURTH.—*Exterior of Birdcage Palace. Flats set immediately behind last scene.*

COMMENCEMENT OF GRAND PLUMED BALLET.

SCENE FIFTH.—*Set of all.*

THE VOLATILE COURT AND ITS PLUMED THRONG.

GRAND BALLET.

END OF THE SECOND ACT.

Characters in Third Act.

VENUS ... ...

ELECTRA ... ...

SATANELLA ... ...

PRINCE LEO ... ...

THE ASTRONOMER-ROYAL ... ...

THE POET LAUREATE ... ...

THE HEREDITARY GRAND MUDDLE

PRINCESS LOTOS-LEAF (*as a Star*) ...

HUBERLU (*as High Priest of Venus*) ...

BABETTE & SISTERS (*as Neophytes*) ...

GOBO ... ...

FIDELIO ... ...

SNOWFLAKE ... ...

The Signs of the Zodiac. Star Visitors of Venus. Characters in the

VISIONS OF PARIS IN SMILES,

AND

PARIS IN TEARS.

ACT III.

SCENE FIRST.—*Horizon and transparency cloths in 1st; the Observatory Terrace by Moonlight, lights down; white lime light on stage; one brilliant star* C. *of cloth thrown by lantern on slides from behind.*

Discovered the ASTRONOMER-ROYAL, *manipulating an astronomical telescope on tripod,* R.C.; LAUREATE *at wing,* R., *and* MUDDLE *at wing,* L., *with small bills in hand; the three wear their former dresses, but now in tatters and patches;* MUDDLE *is now quite bald, and the* LAUREATE *has on a full wig. Music, " Beautiful Star," to open scene.*

LAUR. *and* MUDDLE. Walk up, walk up! Be in time for the transit of Venus. Only ten cents to observe the sidereal phenomenon through the large patent refracting instrument, under the direction of Professor Telescopernicus. Walk up, walk! (*pause*)

LAUR. (*disgusted, coming* R. C.) Not a soul!

MUDDLE. (*coming* L. C.) Not a customer!

ASTRON. Satanella has given us up; Prince Leo has stopped our salaries—and here we are, star-gazing after Lotos-Leaf——

LAUR. Whom we can't find. I have composed a trifle on that. (*clears voice*)
Forgive, blest shade, the tributary tear
That mourns thy exit from a world like this.
Forgive——

THE OTHERS. (*desperately*) No more—no more! Give us poverty and despair, but not that.

LAUR. O, very well. You do so much better, the pair of you. (*suddenly*) Hist! passengers! look out. (*skips to wing,* L.)

THE OTHERS. Ha! (MUDDLE *runs to wing,* R.)

ASTRON. Now then, be in time! Walk up. See the transit of Venus, as she approaches the earth. This is the only genuine telescope, supported by a vote of Congress. Walk up, walk up.

MUDDLE. (*to* ASTRONOMER—*excitedly*) Stop!

ASTRON. Why, who is it then?

(MUDDLE *and* LAUREATE *come* R. *and* L. C. *respectively*)

39

MUDDLE. 'Tis the prince !

THE THREE. (*groaning*) Oh! Oh! (*they huddle behind telescope*).

Enter LEO, GOBO, *and* FIDELIO, R., *in rich tourist dresses.*

LEO. Trusty followers—here on this dizzy height, let us again read the heavens, and seek tidings of Lotos-Leaf.

GOBO. Read the heavens? Oh, oh ! I dont like this kind of literature; besides, we have been reading the heavens to very little purpose. We've got through a few hundred stars, it's true, but there are still some two or three hundred thousand millions more. Don't think of it, master !

LEO. Scoffer !

GOBO. (*sighing*) Babette ! She's not a star, anyhow; not her line of business.

FIDEL. Ah! prince, would your love were not so deep, for much I fear you will never see Lotos-Leaf again.

LEO. (*rapturously*) Never! O, yes—yes, darling, fear not; when we parted, the words of love and not farewell, were on our lips, and a spirit will yet lead me to thee.

[TAKE IN No. 23.]

(*the three* MINISTERS *emerge after song*)

LAUR. *and* MUDDLE. Walk up, walk up—the great telescope—observe the transit of Venus.

ASTRON. Ten cents only, or the lot a quarter. Walk up !

GOBO. Oh, what a rare ragged set.

LEO. Poor fellows, let us give them a turn.

ASTRON. (*adjusting telescope*) This way, sir—place one eye to the orifice and close up the other, and you will see what you shall see.

(FIDELIO *gives money to* LAUREATE—GOBO *looks at his wig and then at* MUDDLE *suspiciously, but can make nothing of it*)

LEO. Why, what is this?

(*Music—the symphony of next number pp. in orchestra, and continued till change of scene*)

OMNES. What ? (ALL *close round him and look up*)

SNOWFLAKE *appears* R., *between wing and cloth, white lime light on her ; she smiles and waves wand ; during next speech the star grows larger until it occupies entire cloth.*

LEO. Amazement! The silver shield opens —it is a vast palace—methinks I see moving multitudes, no bigger than

shining atoms—Ha!—yes—it comes nearer and nearer—the figures grow larger. Oh, wonder! Venus approaches our dark earth.

GOBO. The deuce it does! I'm off.

ASTRON. A collision! let me save my glasses.

OMNES. Ah! (*business*—GOBO *drags* LEO, L., *assisted by* FIDELIO)

FIDEL. Away, prince, away!

LEO. No, no, she may be there.

GOBO. Come! *They exeunt,* L.

LAUR. Oh. dear, oh, dear!

MUDDLE. The end of the world!

ASTRON. At all events I'll save my glasses. (*folds them up*)

LAUR. Stay! a thought.

THE OTHERS. What?

LAUR. I have just composed a little thing——

> Beautiful star, in heaven so bright,
> Softly shines——

THE OTHERS. Come on.

Exeunt, R.—*they drag him off expostulating.*

Enter SNOWFLAKE *immediately,* C. *of stage, clouds down, lime-light on her always.*

SNOW. No end of earth, fond prince; no approximation of distant stars—for lo! earth fades away, and you are lifted high to the arms of Lotos-Leaf.

Retires backwards and slowly off, R., *waving wand— change proceeds rapidly, and discovers*

SCENE SECOND.—*The Heart of a Star;* VENUS *in transit; set; lights up.*

SIGNS OF THE ZODIAC, EVENING, MORNING *and other* STARS *discovered in two lines up stage. Chorus to open scene.*

[TAKE IN No. 24.]

Enter, L. U. E., HUBERLU, *as High Priest of Venus, followed by* BABETTE *and* SISTERS *as Neophytes; they enter singing and range across stage in straight line,* HUBERLU, C.; *immediately the* STARS *and* SIGNS *form large semicircle behind them; chorus over.*

HUBER. Good! I see you have kept your rendezvous. Signs of the changing Zodiac—stars that bring in the night, and herald the morn—bright sentinels that watch every outlet and avenue of the skies—I thank you for this proof of your

fidelity to Plutus, for here, as elsewhere, the dominion of Mammon extends. And ye, brother and sister subjects, ye are faithful still?

OMNES. All!

HUBER. 'Tis well. You know why I have called you together to-day in my character of High Priest of Venus. Not to sacrifice at the shrine of the Goddess of Beauty, but to satisfy the forebodings of Satanella, who believes that Prince Leo, abetted by Snowflake, is daring enough to scale the walls of heaven itself.

OMNES. (*laughing*) Ha, ha!

HUBER. Absurd. But still our loyalty to Satanella demands this caution. Let the chief neophyte call the reports. (*flourish in orchestra*)

BABET. (*with scroll in hand*) Polar Star, what have you seen?

1ST STAR. One grizly and two wrecks. No Leo.

BABET. Guiding Star, has any one sought thy aid?

2ND STAR. No; mortals prefer to walk by their own light. I have seen none. No Leo.

BABET. Morning Star?

3RD STAR. No Leo.

BABET. Evening ditto?

4TH STAR. No Leo.

BABET. O Grand Priest of Venus, the sentinels of the skies make answer that no stranger approaches from the planet called Earth.

OMNES. None!

HUBER. 'Tis well. Lotos-Leaf will become fixed as a star, and so disturb not the reign of our master. (*Music*) Lo! she comes with Venus. (*picture to receive* VENUS)

Enter two CUPIDS, *bearing bow and arrows as avant-couriers,* L. U. E.—VENUS, *leading* LOTOS-LEAF, *and followed by two* CUPID PAGES, *young girls.*

OMNES. Hail, oh Goddess of Beauty.

VENUS. (*merrily*) High priest, I must really ask you to speak to our new star here. There are great complaints amongst the heavenly bodies this morning about her. It seems that instead of quietly remaining in her orbit like a well-conducted young star, she is always rushing off a few million miles into space, with a view it is supposed of getting near that trumpery planet called the Earth. Ridiculous!

HUBER. Quite so.

VENUS. Of all dull, stupid, prosaic planets, that insignificant Earth is the worst.

42

BABET. O decidedly.

OMNES. Certainly.

VENUS. Therefore, sister star, you must be talked to, and broken of this bad habit, which done, I think you will be a credit to our system. By the way, whilst I am on the subject let me ask you to look a little more cheerful. A blinking discontented, sputtering star is not pretty by any means.

LOTOS. Ah! Venus, how *can* I look happy?

VENUS. Follow my example. Love and youth are the elements of all happiness.

LOTOS. And my love is in a far distant sphere.

VENUS. There she goes again! Do speak to her, Pontiff.

HUBER. My daughter, why are you so sad?

LOTOS. Well, if you *will* have it, I don't like being a star. There.

OMNES. (*horrified*) There! there!

HUBER. This is heresy.

LOTOS. I don't care if it is. The life of a star is about the most stupid out. Instead of getting to bed, you have to stick in the cold like a street lamp, and come shivering home in the morning. It is simply disgusting.

VENUS. You are a nice star, upon my word!

LOTOS. But, dear Venus, I have told you that I am not one.

VENUS. Ah! still that fable.

LOTOS. It is no fable. I am an inhabitant of the Earth, and I love, oh, how dearly! one who dwells there.

HUBER. Even were this true, you must forget him—you are separated for ever.

LOTOS. Oh, for pity's sake, don't say that!

(*rolling thunder, soft—tremolo in orchestra—lights begin to be gradually turned down, until the stage is quite dark, to point, afterwards marked*)

VENUS. Ha! what is that?

HUBER. Some of the constellations changing places.

VENUS. I wish they wouldn't. Star showers are coming a great deal too much into fashion again. But see! it is darkening.

OMNES. So it is!

BABET. (R. U. E., *looking off*) Strange! the Earth is approaching rapidly.

VENUS. An eclipse!

BABET. Yes, we are now in its shadow.

OMNES. Ah!

VENUS. What! our kingdom threatened. To me, my friends to me!

43

HUBER. *(aside)* This is still the Power of Love!

(stage dark—tremolo increases to ff.—rolling thunder—the STARS *crouch in circle round* VENUS, *who stands erect,* C., *with* LOTOS-LEAF—*light on them. The* NEOPHYTES *form second ring in front of* VENUS, *bending out with outstretched arms—the* SIGNS OF THE ZODIAC *kneeling in a third circle as if defying foe. This picture exceedingly quick. As soon as it is formed, the thunder stops suddenly, the tremolo stops, and the orchestra play, pp., the phrase of the Duett of First Act, " I love thee, ah, I love thee,"* which LEO *sings off—*LOTOS-LEAF *listens intently, and joins in the ensemble—*SNOWFLAKE *comes on at back, and waves her wand.—on the last note of ensemble,* LEO *rushes on suddenly,* R. 2 E.—*lights on quick—he embraces* LOTOS-LEAF, *and remains in that position, whilst* STARS, NEOPHYTES, &c., *form fresh picture round stage)*

Enter FIDELIO, GOBO, *and the* THREE MINISTERS, R.—*chords, ff. and Music stops.*

VENUS. What has happened? (SNOWFLAKE *comes down,* C.)*

SNOW. Let an old friend answer.

VENUS. Ah, Snowflake!

SNOW. Yes, goddess, in the dark planet that has just passed by your palace of light, it is not enough that your gifts of love and beauty should be given to mortals—there are thousand foes to guard even the innocent against, and to that task I have devoted myself.

VENUS. Then these are lovers?

LEO. O, goddess, none ever worshipped more fervently at thy shrine.

VENUS. Then must I protect my votaries. Be happy.

LOTOS. Kind Venus! *(they go up)*

HUBER. *(aside)* Confusion! Once more foiled.

GOBO. There's a star over there winking at me. *(business with* BABETTE) Yes—no—yes—why—*(crosses)* I say, Bab——

BABET. Sir!

GOBO. I beg your pardon. *(business)* Let me reflect.

ASTRON. My telescope has done it.

MUDDLE. No; my diplomacy.

---

	* MINISTERS.		BABETTE.		
GOBO.					SISTERS.
FIDELIO.					HUBERLU.
	SNOWFLAKE.	LEO.	LOTOS-LEAF.	VENUS.	
R.					L.

44

LAUR. What a chance for a poem. Like this—(*clears voice*)

Twinkle, twinkle little star,
How I wonder what you are,
Up above the world so high——

Shall I continue?

OMNES. No, no! (*he is crushed—the others come down in line for finale*)

VENUS. Then let us celebrate what is dearest to me—the union of two faithful hearts. Nectar there—green seal.

(*the four* CUPIDS *who have been off, give quickly cups to* PRINCIPALS)

[TAKE IN No. 25.]

SCENE SECOND.—*Cloth in 1st; the Boudoir of Venus; lights full up.*

Enter HUBERLU *and* NEOPHYTES.

HUBER. This is a pleasant arrival for us, girls.

BABET. Well, papa, if you must know what I think, allow me to observe that Snowflake is too many for us.

THE OTHERS. Evidently.

BABET. And that the sooner we return home the better. (*aside*) Fact is, the sight of Gobo has been too much for me!

HUBER. (*in despair*) What is to be done?—What is to be done?

Trap Music—enter by trap, C., ELECTRA, *to take up cue immediately.*

ELECTRA. Resign!

OMNES. Ah!

ELECTRA. Yes—Plutus has just sent me up to say that your talents will grace retirement better than his active service.

HUBER. Despair!

BABET. (*aside*) Rapture!

HUBER. Then the pursuit of Leo and Lotos-Leaf is abandoned?

ELECTRA. That I know not. What is certain is, that you will not be in at the death.

HUBER. Can Satanella find better servants?

ELECTRA. Ask her?

45

Enter SATANELLA, L.

SATANEL. And she replies—yes. (*all salaam humbly*) You think me defeated? No; but I own that I under-rated the power opposed to me. Had I not done so, I should scarcely have chosen tools like you. Meanwhile, like a desperate general, who, to retrieve the failing fortunes of a fight, urges his steed into the front of battle, so do I—and mark me, I shall win.

BABET. Hist! Here comes Venus and her guests!

SATANEL. Now for stratagem.

Phrase of Chorus of last scene. Enter VENUS, LOTOS-LEAF, MINISTERS, FIDELIO, GOBO, STARS, *and* SIGNS OF ZODIAC, R.,—*picture.*

LOTOS. (*starting*) Ha!

OMNES. What?

LOTOS. The Evil Spirit! (*clinging to* LEO)

VENUS. Who, sister?

LOTOS. Satanella!

OMNES. Ah!

LEO. Back, fiend, thou shall not bewitch her!

VENUS. (*proudly*) Power of mischance! and thou hast dared to wage thy iniquitous warfare, even on my threshold?

SATANEL. (*assuming humble air*) No, great Venus, not in arms I come, but suppliant. Hear me, Prince! Hear that penitence can attain to such a heart as mine.

LEO. Strange!

HUBER. (*aside*) Can such things be?

SATANEL. Then, behold in me, henceforth, a friend—or if that position be denied me, a defeated foe who can bow her head before beauty and virtue!

VENUS. Can we believe this change?

(SATANELLA *has meanwhile motioned rapidly to the three* MINISTERS)

MUDDLE. It appears to me genuine.

ASTRON. Fallen stars are not less stars, and may resume their orbit.

LAUR. As I once remarked on a similar occasion (*clearing voice*)

> To err is human, to forgive, divine,
> And so, dear friends——

OMNES. No—no!

LAUR. (*disgusted*) Oh! of course not!

LEO. I do accept thy penitence, Satanella.

LOTOS. And I—I forgive thee all the ill thou hast done.

OMNES. Bravo!

46

SATANEL. Let me now give an earnest of what I have promised. First let me expose the toils that still cling around you. Let me unmask the wicked Huberlu where he stands. (*pointing to* HUBERLU)

OMNES. Ha!

HUBER. Traitress!

SATANEL. (*smiling*) Fool! Return to thy ravine in Brittany.

GOBO. Brittany! Huberlu?

SATANEL. And you, Neophytes, take again thy shapes as his daughters.

GOBO. Daughters! (*looking at* BABETTE)

BABET. Oh, I'm so glad, Gobo.

GOBO. Babette! (*they embrace*)

VENUS. (*to* HUBERLU) Quit my sphere this day—ignoble sorcerer—never to return.

HUBER. (*aside*) This is to serve a fiend!

SATANEL. One proof more of my friendship: when again you return to earth a happy pair, let Satanella offer you a marriage gift. She places at your disposal, for your wedding tour, all that is brightest and loveliest below; a spot consecrated to love and pleasure—where nought exists that hath affinity to sorrow.

LOTOS. O, where is that spot?

SATANEL. It is called by mortals, Paris.

OMNES. Paris!

VENUS. And yet methinks I have heard from my votaries in that distant sphere, that a song of joy has there ended in a burden of sorrow.

SATANEL. Calumny, great Venus—calumny! But I will be honest to the uttermost. Would you, as in a magic mirror gaze upon this Paris?

OMNES. Yes—yes!

SATANEL. Then you shall.

Music in orchestra to discover Fête Scene at St. Cloud—she waves wand—the CROWD *separates into entrances—the cloth goes and discovers*

SCENE FOURTH.—ST. CLOUD EN FÊTE; *variety business.* PARIS IN SMILES, *closed in by*

SCENE FIFTH.—*Repeat Scene 3rd.*

Re-enter all the PERSONAGES *who were on at the end of Scene 3rd; same picture;* SATANELLA, C.

SATANEL. Well, said I not right. Is not Paris the chosen home of pleasure and of love?

LEO. Good spirit, Paris for me.

47

LOTOS. And for me.

OMNES. And for all of us!

VENUS. I confess I had no idea that my own ideas were so thoroughly carried out in that dim and distant planet.

SATANEL. Then, Prince, you accept my offer?

LEO. O, with rapture!

SATANEL. (*aside, with fiendish glee*) Then all is not lost! (*aloud*) En route, then, dear friends, and let us bid farewell to our hostess, great Venus!

Enter SNOWFLAKE, R.

SNOW. One moment!

LOTOS. Our good spirit!

SATANEL. (*aside*) Confusion—she again!

SNOW. Dear Venus, and you my stupid young protégés, I really find I have to act as a sort of guardian to goddesses and mortals alike. You don't mean to say that you believe what you have just seen?

VENUS. Why, Snowflake, we have eyes!

LEO. Yes, and we have seen a reality, have we not?

SATANEL. Certainly.

SNOW. No—you have not.

SATANEL. I defy you to the proof!

SNOW. Ah, my ancient enemy, this new stratagem like the others, will fail, for by my power, I will show the reverse of the medal—the dark side of the picture you have so cunningly pourtrayed. (*to* LEO) When I have done so, say then whether Paris is the place you would take your bride to. You have seen Paris in smiles—be it mine to show you Paris in tears! (*waving wand*) Behold!

(*Music in orchestra—the characters back into entrances*, R. *and* L., *as before—the cloth goes—discovering*

SCENE SIXTH.—PARIS IN TEARS! *Panorama of the City under the Commune.*

END OF THE THIRD ACT.

48

ACT IV.

SCENE FIRST.—*Dark Clouds in 1st. A Cloud Corridor in the Halls of Venus.*

Discovered, VENUS *and her* CUPID PAGES; HUBERLU *and* DAUGHTERS *in 1st costumes;* PRINCE *and* PRINCESS *in 2nd ditto;* GOBO *in 2nd ditto;* FIDELIO *in 1st ditto;* MINISTERS *in 1st ditto;* ELECTRA, KING *and* QUEEN JEWEL *in 1st ditto, and a selection of other* CHARACTERS *to dress stage. No dialogue. They sing next concerted piece.*

[TAKE IN No. 26.]

Then divide CHARACTERS, *and pass to*

SCENE SECOND.—GRAND TRANSFORMATION SCENE!

THE NATIVITY OF VENUS.

Curtain.

Printed by THOMAS SCOTT, 1, Warwick Court, Holborn.